100 Pounds of Popcorn

100 Pounds of
Popcorn

by Hazel Krantz

Illustrations by Vic Herman

SCHOLASTIC BOOK SERVICES
NEW YORK • TORONTO • LONDON • AUCKLAND • SYDNEY • TOKYO

ISBN: 0-590-00142-6

Copyright © 1961 by Hazel Krantz. This edition is published by Scholastic Book Services, a division of Scholastic Magazines, Inc., by arrangement with Vanguard Press, Inc.

16 15 14 13 12

1 2 3/8
11

Printed in U.S.A.

Contents

The
Big
Find

It ALL BEGAN one hot Saturday afternoon in July. The Taylors' car was crawling along the Harrison Turnpike, stuck in the middle of a traffic jam. The car smelled of salt from wet bathing suits. There was sand all over the floor. There were cars in front and cars in back, all filled with mothers and fathers and children and wet, sandy bathing suits.

"It just takes all the pleasure out of a day at the beach," complained Mrs. Taylor, trying to sweep away some of the sand with her fingers, "getting caught in a traffic jam like this."

Mr. Taylor leaned back and just twiddled with the steering wheel. He did not say anything, but his mouth was a straight, unhappy line as he kept taking his foot off and then putting it back on the gas pedal. Finally he muttered, "How about having a drink of lemonade?"

Mrs. Taylor turned the spigot on the lemonade jug. One little drop fell into the paper cup. "Empty," she said, as if everyone couldn't see that.

1

"May we stop for frozen custard?" asked eight-year-old Sally Jean, who generally said the wrong thing.

"Quiet!" said Mr. Taylor impatiently.

"Now, now, Joseph," said Mrs. Taylor. "After all, it's nobody's fault. Sally Jean, you should know we can't stop for frozen custard in the middle of a traffic jam."

Andy Taylor, who was eleven years old, craned his neck out the window and looked at the cars in the back and the cars in the front, and tried to think of a plan. Andy always liked to figure things out.

He wrinkled his brow and poked his nose out into the hot wind. It occurred to him that he and his father could buy a used helicopter propeller and put it on the roof of the car for just such an occasion. But that plan, while excellent, would not do for the present. He needed a plan for right now.

Then he noticed that all the cars were on the Harrison Turnpike. There were hardly any cars on the side roads.

"Why don't we turn off the turnpike and go around by the side roads?" said Andy, ducking his head back into the car.

"No, no, no!" cried Mrs. Taylor. "We'll only get lost."

"Nonsense," said Mr. Taylor, his blue eyes happy at the thought of getting off the Turnpike. "I have an excellent sense of direction. Old Bird-Dog Taylor they used to call me in the Army." And with that, he gripped the steering wheel and made a wide turn. The car whisked around a corner and out of the line of cars and onto a rutty, dusty, narrow country road.

The car sailed along, past cows flicking their tails lazily in the shade, past barking dogs, past barns and houses.

"This is more like it," said Mr. Taylor happily.

"Where does this road go?" asked Mrs. Taylor.

"To Mepham," said Mr. Taylor confidently. "It winds around and then it picks up the Turnpike again just before Mepham."

"How do you know?" asked Mrs. Taylor.

"Don't you remember this road? We were here last spring. That yellow house with the two poplar trees?"

"No," said Mrs. Taylor. "I don't remember ever seeing that house before."

"Maybe they painted it," said Mr. Taylor.

"Look out, Dad," shouted Andy. "There's a truck."

A rickety truck piled high with fat burlap bags pulled out of a road ahead of them. Mr. Taylor slowed down and they crept along behind the truck. "Just our luck," said Mr. Taylor disgustedly. "The truck has a whole road to ride on, and it has to get in front of us."

He zigzagged the car to the left, but the road was too narrow for passing. He honked the horn, but the truck would not move over. It just lumbered along, with the Taylors' car trailing behind.

Suddenly the truck went over a rut and one of the fat burlap bags bounced off and lay in the road. Mr. Taylor stopped the car and got out. Andy clambered out after him.

"Hey," they yelled to the back of the truck. "You lost something!"

But the truck just rumbled and snorted, sent a cloud of dust into their eyes, and disappeared down another country road.

"Help me get this thing out of the way," puffed Mr. Taylor to Andy. "It must weigh a hundred pounds."

"Let's see what's inside," said Andy, working his finger into the bag. It came out with a little hard kernel of corn. "Chicken feed," Andy decided.

Mr. Taylor squinted at a faded-looking label on the side of the bag. "It's not chicken feed," he said. "It's popping corn."

Andy looked at the label. Sure enough, it said "Popping Corn, 100 pounds."

One hundred pounds of popping corn! Andy started jumping up and down, and Sally Jean got out of the car and jumped up and down too.

"Not so fast," said Mr. Taylor. "This popping corn belongs to someone. We have to try to find out who."

He turned the bag over. On the back it was labeled "Star Popcorn Company."

A farmer who was hoeing his rows of corn in a field near the road ambled over to see what the excitement was about. He looked at the children.

"Well, I see someone who likes popcorn," he grinned.

"That's all very well," said Mrs. Taylor, who had gotten out of the car. "But this popcorn belongs to the Star Popcorn Company — not to us. It's only right that we let them know we found it."

The farmer leaned on his hoe. "That's right," he commented. "I know that outfit. Belongs to Jim Ferguson, who lives about a mile from here. Why don't you call him up? I'd be glad to let you use my telephone."

Mr. Taylor went into the farmer's house, with Andy trailing behind. He dialed Mr. Ferguson's number. A voice answered, "Hello, Jim Ferguson speaking."

"My name's Taylor," said Mr. Taylor. "One of your trucks was driving in front of us and lost a hundred-pound bag of popcorn. It's over near" — he looked at the farmer, who said, "My name's Billings." "It's next to Billings' farm," Mr. Taylor continued.

"Oh," said Mr. Ferguson. "That must be Gus's truck. He's on his way to the city, and there's no way I can get him to come back for it. I'm in bed with a

bad back myself. By the time we could get it, it would probably spoil, lying in the road that way. But I don't like to leave it in the middle of the road. Traffic hazard, you know."

"Don't worry about that," replied Mr. Taylor. "My son and I will move it out of the way for you."

"That's mighty nice of you," said Mr. Ferguson. "Say, you wouldn't want to keep the popcorn for yourself, would you? That would save me the trouble of coming for it."

"That's very generous of you," said Mr. Taylor.

"Not at all," said Mr. Ferguson. "You are doing me a real favor if you take it."

Mr. Taylor put down the telephone. "Well," he said, "I guess it's ours if we want it. But I can't imagine what we are going to do with so much popping corn. We couldn't eat it in a year."

"Please, Dad," begged Andy, "can't we keep it?"

"All right, all right," said Mr. Taylor. "But I know what will happen. It'll just take up space in the garage and get all wormy."

Andy and his father tugged and heaved, and put the bag into the trunk of the car. After that, Andy was so busy making plans about what he was going to do with the popcorn that he hardly noticed when the road they were on ended in a cabbage field instead of going to Mepham. All the time his father was making U turns and trying one road after another looking for the Harrison Turnpike again, thoughts were reeling around in Andy's head, like a top. He wasn't going to leave the popcorn in the garage. He was going to pop it and sell it at fifteen cents a bag. He could see himself becoming richer and richer.

"About how many bags of popcorn can you get to a pound of popping corn, Dad?" he asked.

"About fifteen," said Mr. Taylor absent-mindedly as he peered at a road sign. "Looks like the right road at last."

"Anybody want a sandwich?" asked Mrs. Taylor, producing a sandy one from the picnic basket.

Andy took the sandwich and brushed it off with his hand as he tried to figure out how much he could make on the popcorn. His fifth-grade teacher said he was a whiz at arithmetic, but fifteen cents times fifteen bags times a hundred pounds got all tangled up, so he asked his mother for a pencil. He figured it out on the back of a bag.

"Wow!" he shouted. "Two hundred and twenty-five dollars!"

"I want two hundred and twenty-five dollars too," demanded Sally Jean.

"You may each have $112.50 apiece," said Mrs. Taylor quietly. She was a very fair woman.

Andy wrinkled his brow and looked at his sister,

who was eating a banana. "Well," he said, "if she's going to be my partner, she's got to help me make the popcorn and sell it."

All the time they were on the Harrison Turnpike again, back in the traffic jam, Andy tried to think of a good way to spend the $112.50. Boy, you could buy a car for that much money! But, he thought sadly, it would be years before he would be old enough to drive it. A new bike? A big chemistry set to make his own atomic power? A telescope like the one at Mount Palomar with which to look at outer space?

Sally Jean was thinking too. "I'm going to buy a queen doll," she said. "With a golden crown and a real fur coat."

"When we get home," said Mrs. Taylor, "I want you both to take good hot showers. Make sure all the sand and salt are out of your hair."

Andy, who was looking out the window and seeing himself as a famous scientist with his own observatory in his back yard, sighed. "Mothers," he thought. "At a moment like this all they think about is a good hot shower!"

Partners

THE NEXT MORNING Andy made one telephone call, to his friend Barry Lindhoffer, to tell him about the popping corn. Before he knew it, the Taylor garage was packed with boys and girls, all looking at the burlap bag. Almost the whole Westville Little League was there, and Sally Jean's entire Brownie troop. They all wanted to be partners of the Taylor children in the popcorn business.

"You need salesmen," argued Weenie Jackson.

"Yeah, you sure do," echoed Barry.

"You have to have someone to help make the popcorn," said Peggy Marshall, who had braids that bounced up and down whenever she talked.

Andy looked at the mob of boys and girls and thought about sharing his $112.50 with them. The first thing he wanted to do was to tell them all to go away. This was his and Sally Jean's private popcorn.

But then he looked at the fat burlap bag, bulging with popping corn. He and Sally Jean could never pop all that corn and sell it by themselves. They needed help.

"All right," he said finally. "We'll let four more into the business."

"Me! Me! Me!" shouted the children.

Andy picked Weenie because he was the best pitcher on the Westville team, and Barry because he was Andy's best friend.

Meanwhile Sally Jean's friends were hopping around her like Mexican jumping beans.

"Now you pick two girls," said Andy.

Sally Jean's first choice was easy. Sally Jean and Peggy Marshall always did everything together, so of course Peggy could help with the popcorn.

"Sally Jean, if you don't let me be a partner I'll never speak to you again," sniffed Bonnie Singleton, wiggling her shoulders and shaking her pony tail as she always did when she wanted something.

Sally Jean really didn't like Bonnie very much, but she knew what Bonnie did when she was angry. She went around whispering mean things about a person. Sally Jean felt her face getting hot under the freckles. Then she pointed at Bonnie.

After the rest of the children had gone home, the partners rushed into Mrs. Taylor's kitchen, where Mr.

and Mrs. Taylor were drinking coffee and reading the Sunday newspaper.

"How do you make popcorn, Mom?" shouted Andy and Sally Jean.

"Well," said Mrs. Taylor, "you take a little oil and put it into a heavy iron pot with a cover. Then you put the popping corn — not too much — into the oil. When you hear the popcorn banging around, you know it's finished. Then you put some salt and butter on it."

"Um, yum, yum," said Andy and Sally Jean and their friends.

"Where's the oil? Where's the butter? Where's a nice heavy pot?"

"All right, children," smiled Mrs. Taylor, putting down the book review section of the newspaper, "I guess you can make a little popcorn. Just so long as you don't spoil your lunch."

She took out her big iron chicken-frying pan and a small bottle of cooking oil and a piece of butter.

Andy looked at the supplies doubtfully. "Mother, he said, "do you think this is enough . . . I mean enough to pop the whole hundred pounds of corn?"

Mrs. Taylor nearly dropped the frying pan. "You mean to say," she said, "that you are going to pop a hundred pounds of corn — right here, now, in *my* kitchen?"

"Of course," replied Andy. "We *told* you we were going into business. We're going to make two hundred and twenty-five dollars. We *told* you!"

Mr. Taylor laid the sports section on the table. He took off his glasses and wiped them. Then he put on his serious look, which meant that two straight lines appeared on his forehead.

"Am I to understand that you are going into business?" he asked.

"Yes, sir," replied Andy.

Mr. Taylor drummed on the table with his glasses. "Hum," he said thoughtfully. Then he said, "If you are going to sell the popcorn for profit, you can't expect to get the raw materials for nothing. After all, in my storm-window business, I must buy the aluminum and glass before I can make the storm windows. It's only fair that a popcorn company should buy its own butter and oil."

Andy sat down on the step stool and thought about that. He certainly didn't want his father to think he wasn't a real businessman.

"About how much do you think the . . . the raw materials will cost, Dad?" he asked.

Mr. Taylor looked up at the ceiling and did some mental figuring. "Well, you already have the popping corn," he said. "That's a saving. The oil and butter should run to about ten dollars, roughly speaking.

"Of course, you don't need all that capital at once, you know. You can work with what we call 'revolving capital' — start with two dollars and sell some of your product, and with the profit buy more materials to make more product, and with the profit from that buy more mat — "

Andy bit his lip. He really didn't care about revolving capital. All he knew was that sooner or later he would need $10, so he might as well get it right now.

Then he thought of something. "Would you lend us the money, Dad?" he asked.

"Certainly," said Mr. Taylor. "What can you put up for collateral?"

"Col . . . what?" asked Andy.

"Collateral. When you borrow money from a bank, they always ask you for collateral. That means you put up something they can take if you don't pay them back. The bank loaned us money to buy this house. If we didn't pay them back, a little each month, they could take away the house. Now, if I were in the grain business, I would take the corn itself for collateral. After all, you can't pop it all at once, and what's left would be worth quite a lot of money. But since I'm not, I'm afraid you'll have to think of something else."

Andy looked at his father as if he had changed into

a strange new creature. He was not a father at all. He was a human bank! "You're mean!" he said.

"Not at all," said Mr. Taylor, putting his glasses back on again and picking up the sports section. "After all, I'm not charging you interest. The bank does, you know. You have to pay them extra for using their money."

Andy and Sally Jean took their friends upstairs to help them look for collateral. All Sally Jean could find was a doll crib with the sides coming off. Andy had some old comic books and some baseball cards. He had some model planes with parts missing. He also had his baseball bat and mitt.

Weenie picked up Andy's baseball mitt. "This should be worth something," he said.

Andy grabbed the mitt from Weenie. He fingered the oily leather lovingly. Andy babied that mitt. Once a week he oiled it to keep it nice and soft.

He put his fist into the palm and thought about how he had worked over that pocket, tying a baseball inside the mitt and pressing it with weights to get it just right.

A terrible thought occurred to him. Supposing, after he had borrowed the money from his father and made the popcorn, no one wanted to buy it? Then his father could take the mitt away. Tears almost came to his eyes at the frightening scene of himself, without a mitt, going down to Little League practice.

"No," he said, sitting down on his bed and hugging the mitt to his chest. "There must be some other way to do it."

"Well," said Barry, "we could always earn the money the way we shoveled snow for Christmas presents."

"How can you shovel snow, stupid?" asked Weenie. "It's July."

"We could weed," said Sally Jean.

"That's a good idea," said Andy. "We'll all go out and get jobs weeding people's gardens, cutting the grass, washing cars. There are millions of jobs. We can start tomorrow."

"Well, I don't know," said Weenie slowly. "I have to practice my pitching."

"I have to go to the dentist tomorrow," said Peggy.

"Look," said Andy desperately, "you've got to help me. I'll give you equal shares in the money we make selling the popcorn."

"Oh," said Weenie, "that's different. I guess I can practice Tuesday."

"I'll be back from the dentist at two o'clock," promised Peggy.

Workers For Hire

MONDAY AFTERNOON, the six children divided up into pairs and went around the neighborhood ringing doorbells and asking for work. It was amazing how many people did not need their gardens weeded or their cars washed.

Then the weather started to get really hot, and the group began to think of all the nice cool things they could be doing instead of tramping up and down the street ringing doorbells. They could be sitting under the trees having a picnic. They could be wading in the Cherry Avenue brook. They could be fishing.

Andy and Barry trudged up the walk to Mrs. Desmond's house. Neither of them said anything, but they were each thinking that if Mrs. Desmond didn't want any work done, they would give up and go home.

Mrs. Desmond looked hot and cross when she answered the door. From somewhere in the house they could hear a baby crying.

"Pardon me, ma'am," said Andy politely. "We're gardeners. Would you like your garden weeded?"

19

Mrs. Desmond sighed. She gave the boys a long look. "The garden *is* full of weeds. And I don't have time to weed it. Maybe . . ."

"We'll work cheap," said Barry quickly. "Real cheap."

Mrs. Desmond smiled. "Well, if you don't charge too much . . ."

"Oh no," said Andy. "We're the most reasonable gardeners in town. Would twenty-five cents each for the whole yard be too much?"

"I think that would be fair," said Mrs. Desmond slowly. "But be sure you don't pull up any flowers by mistake."

After the Desmond yard had been weeded, business picked up. Mrs. Desmond had a friend who needed her garden weeded too. Mrs. McGinnis had to go to the drugstore, so she hired Sally Jean to stay with her baby. Peggy walked Mrs. Anderson's dog. Bonnie helped Mrs. Atkins sweep up her back patio. Weenie washed Mrs. Bailey's car, all by himself.

Soon the whole neighborhood knew about the helpful children. The Taylors' telephone started ringing, and Mrs. Taylor had to keep taking messages about jobs.

Late in the afternoon the children gathered in the Taylors' back yard. They were so hot and tired they felt they would melt away. The boys sat on the grass

instead of bothering to take their usual places in the branches of the apple tree.

Mrs. Taylor brought out lemonade. "Well," she said, "did you earn the ten dollars?"

Andy counted out the quarters and dimes they had earned. They had just two dollars. "Gosh," he said, "it's hard to earn money. We worked a long time for two dollars. It'll take us forever to make ten."

Mrs. Taylor brought out the list of jobs that had come in over the telephone. "Don't be discouraged," she said. "There are two more cars to be washed, three dogs to be walked, and a lawn to be mowed. Mrs. Gates is giving a lawn party. She wants a girl to come and help serve refreshments."

The partners groaned. Weenie started turning his pitching arm in circles. "It's stiff," he complained. "I strained it reaching to the roof of the Baileys' car."

Andy and Barry anxiously rubbed Weenie's arm. They had to be careful of that pitching arm. There was to be a big game against Midland Valley the next Saturday.

"There's only one answer," said Andy unwillingly. "We need more help."

"That means we have to share the popcorn money with more people," said Barry.

"I know," Andy replied, rubbing away at Weenie's arm. He divided $225 by six in his head. That came to $37.50 — his share if the money was divided equally among the partners he already had. He scratched his head and divided again. It was still $37.50. He felt as if his money were disappearing. It was hard to think of $37.50 when you were used to thinking of $112.50. But he knew that if he didn't have the other boys and girls to help him, he would never be able to sell any popcorn at all. Then he would have nothing.

"We've got to have some more people to do all that work," said Weenie. "How about two more Brownies and two other fellows from the team?"

Andy chewed on a piece of grass as he divided the $225 again, this time by ten. He groaned. It came to only $22.50 per person!

But it couldn't be helped. They had to have more people. "Okay," he said, sighing. "We'll ask two more girls and two more boys. But that's all. No more partners after that!"

Andy thought again about the $22.50. It wasn't so bad, really. Maybe he couldn't buy a big telescope, but he could buy a small one — just right for a beginning astronomer like himself.

Popcorn, Popcorn Everywhere

It was a good thing that the Taylor Popcorn Company, as the partners had named their business, added four more members. After the ten dollars for the butter and oil had been earned, someone remembered they needed bags in which to put the popcorn. Still more lawns had to be mowed and dogs to be walked to pay for all this.

When Andy, Barry, and Weenie, the bag committee, went down to the five-and-ten and asked for fifteen hundred large-sized sandwich bags, at first the salesgirl thought they were fooling. Then she called Mr. Jensen, the manager.

Mr. Jensen was very serious when they told him they were in business.

"Since you are not regular retail customers," he said, "we'd better go into my office. Then we can talk like businessmen."

Mr. Jensen was a tall young man. He had a thoughtful look on his face. Andy and Barry and Weenie liked him, for he did not treat them as if they were just children.

24

Andy explained about the hundred pounds of popping corn. Mr. Jensen was very interested. He sold popcorn, too. He gave them advice about keeping the popcorn clean. "No one will buy merchandise that is not fresh and clean," he explained. "Especially if it is something to eat.

"I'll tell you what, boys," he added. "I'll give you the dealer's price on the bags. You can have them for just what they cost me."

"Gosh, thanks," said Andy.

"Not at all," replied Mr. Jensen. He stood up and shook hands with each of the boys.

Now that the partners had earned enough money to buy the butter, oil, and paper bags they needed, the real job began. "Production," as Andy's father called it. This was another way of saying it was time to make the popcorn.

The popcorn factory was located in the Taylor kitchen. But very soon it became clear that Mrs. Taylor's chicken-frying pan would never be able to make fifteen hundred bags of popcorn fast enough. It was also a fact that Mrs. Taylor sometimes needed her kitchen for other uses, such as making dinner.

It was getting very hot and crowded, with ten partners sitting and dangling around in the kitchen. One day, as Mrs. Taylor was trying to put some lamb chops into the broiler, Weenie nearly gave her a shampoo with hot oil.

"*Eeee,*" screamed Mrs. Taylor, backing away in a hurry and dropping the lamb chops on the floor.

Andy felt just awful as he stooped to help his mother pick up the chops. His mother had been just as nice as anyone could be to him and his partners, but he could see how much they were bothering her. Her curly brown hair was stringy from the heat of all the cooking, and she looked as if she were ready to cry.

Suddenly the screen door twanged open and Mr. Taylor stood in the doorway of the kitchen. He just stood very quietly, staring at the mess. Then he said, "I think it's time for everyone to go home."

The partners thought so too. Silently they cleaned up the popcorn-making equipment and filed out.

Andy followed his father into the living room. Mr. Taylor was glancing at a magazine. Andy sat on the arm of his father's chair and swung one leg back and forth.

"It was a dumb idea to go into the popcorn business, huh, Dad?"

Mr. Taylor put the magazine down on the coffee table and took out his pipe. "What makes you think so?" he asked.

"Well, we're bothering Mom, and we worked all afternoon and only got five bags filled. It's a mess."

"True," said Mr. Taylor. "It's a mess the way you're doing it now. But that's no reason to quit. When a businessman sees that his production methods are wrong, he tries to figure out something better he can do that will improve the situation."

Andy looked out a window at some bumblebees chasing one another around a honeysuckle vine. Somehow they reminded him of his partners and himself, just going around in circles without any real plans. He thought hard about what was wrong. Then he started to have some ideas about how to fix things.

"We should only pop corn in the morning, when Mom doesn't need the kitchen so much," he offered as a starter.

"Good," said Mr. Taylor.

"We shouldn't have so many people in the kitchen at one time," Andy decided.

"Excellent," commented Mr. Taylor.

"But Dad, if only a few of us work at a time, it'll take forever to make enough popcorn to sell," Andy complained.

"Why don't you subcontract?" asked Mr. Taylor.

"What's 'subcontract'?" asked Andy.

"When a manufacturer doesn't have the space or equipment to make his entire product, he lets some other factory do it," he explained. "In other words, use some of your partners' kitchens too."

Andy's partners thought this was a wonderful idea. It took quite a lot of talking to some of the other

POPCORN
15¢

mothers, but finally the Taylor Popcorn Company found itself operating in three kitchens.

The partners divided up the work. Some of them popped corn. Some put it into bags. Some carted in more corn from the big burlap bag.

The popcorn smelled good as it banged and rattled away in the pots. It reminded you of the circus and the movies and a day at the beach. It tasted good, too. At first everybody grabbed big handfuls of popcorn as soon as it came out of the pan. The bag committee kept complaining that they weren't getting enough to fill their bags.

Then the partners stopped eating the popcorn. Somehow they just weren't hungry for it. And the smell of it was terrible. It had become such a popcorny smell!

Andy and Barry went down to the supermarket and brought back cardboard cartons in which to store the finished popcorn. Soon the cartons were overflowing. But the burlap bag was still round and fat with unpopped corn.

Then Andy remembered something very important. He remembered what Mr. Jensen had said about keeping the merchandise fresh and clean.

"Stop!" he shouted.

Sally Jean's hand stopped in mid-air just as she was about to pour some fresh corn into the pan.

"We can't make any more," Andy said excitedly.

"At least not today. It will spoil. Let's first sell what we have and make some more when that's gone."

The partners stacked the bags of popcorn into express wagons and walked up and down the street. They took turns calling, "Popcorn! Nice fresh popcorn! Fifteen cents a bag."

At first business was not so good. But when they lowered the price to ten cents, it improved. All the children in the neighborhood ran out and begged their mothers to buy popcorn. Before the afternoon was over, every single white bag had disappeared from the popcorn carts. The ten partners had a bag of dimes to jingle happily.

They decided to invest some of their money in ice-cream sodas.

"Boy," said Andy, poking his straw into a corner of the glass to get some chocolate syrup he had missed, "making money is a cinch this way. Let's start real early tomorrow."

The next day and the next, the partners worked hard. All morning they made popcorn and all afternoon they sold it. They walked farther and farther with their carts, and they sold popcorn to people they had never seen before.

Then, on the fourth day, people started shaking their heads when they heard the cry, "Nice fresh popcorn!" It seemed that the whole town was tired of popcorn.

The partners gathered under the apple tree for a conference. They took off their shoes and rested their aching feet. They looked at the carts still filled with white bags.

"We've run out of customers," said Andy sadly.

Everyone sat around with his chin in his hand, thinking. Only Weenie couldn't sit still. Weenie could never stay quiet. He wandered off and started exercising his pitching arm. He rocked back on his heels, squinted his eyes, and aimed a rock at the fence.

Andy looked at him, admiring his form. Then a great bright light turned on in his head.

He snapped his fingers. "Hey," he said. "Baseball game! Popcorn! Everybody eats popcorn at a baseball game. We'll sell it at the Little League game with Midland Valley on Saturday!"

Barry jumped to his feet. "Not only popcorn," he shouted. "We'll use the money we've made and buy hot dogs and soda. We'll have a real concession."

"Sure," cried Andy. "That's a great idea."

Then he thought a minute. He looked at Sally Jean and Peggy and Bonnie and the other two Brownies. They were the ones who would have to do the selling, because the boys would be playing ball. He could just imagine them trying to sell hot dogs and soda *and* popcorn.

"I think," he said slowly, "we'd better just stick to popcorn."

The Baseball Game

SATURDAY turned out to be bright and sunny. The bleachers at the high school field were filled with parents and sisters and brothers from Westville and Midland Valley. Sally Jean and her Brownie friends climbed up and down the bleacher steps yelling "Popcorn! Popcorn! Ten cents a bag." They had clothespin bags tied around their waists in which to keep the change.

But the boys had more to think about than popcorn just now. That Midland Valley team was tough. Their outfield caught Westville's balls like flypaper. Their hitters whanged away at Weenie's fast balls as if they were marshmallows.

By the beginning of the second inning, Midland Valley had three runs to Westville's nothing. But in the top of the second inning, Westville started to fight back. Jim Benson came in for a run. Then in the third inning, Tommy Engel hit a two-bagger, sending two men home.

With the score tied, the two teams battled through the fourth inning, neither one giving an inch. From far away came the roar of the parents in the stands. But on the field only one thing was important: to play ball!

At the bottom of the fifth inning, Westville was out in the field, with Andy holding down center field. There were no outs and no runs. Two men were on base.

Big Paddy Ryan swaggered up to the plate. The Westville boys eyed him tensely. They knew this Ryan. He was powerful, but wild. He was likely to hit a pop fly. He was also likely to hit a home run.

Mr. Coogan, the Westville coach, signaled Andy to play deep. But Andy didn't need to be told. He knew Paddy Ryan's hits had a way of winging all the way to the fence in back of center field.

As Weenie wound up for a fancy curve ball, Andy felt the good firm pocket in his glove. His hand itched for the slap of Ryan's hit against his mitt. To his right, Jerry Margolis crouched down, eying the plate, his nose quivering a little.

The play Mr. Coogan had taught them for just such a situation clicked through Andy's mind. Taylor to grab the fly ball, throw to Margolis. Margolis throws to Benson on third to tag the runner coming in from second. With luck, a nice double play.

Weenie threw the curve. It went spiraling over the plate. Strike one! Shrieks and boos went up from the crowd, depending on which side they were for.

Ryan banged the plate with his bat and eyed Weenie. Then he planted his feet firmly apart and held the bat ready, his muscles tense with power.

Weenie threw a fast one. The ball went right over the plate. Ryan hit it a mighty whack and the ball sailed right down toward center field.

Suddenly Andy heard a loud wail from the stands. Sally Jean! He recognized her voice and out of the corner of his eye saw what was happening. Sally Jean had been trying to give people change when they bought popcorn. But with all the excitement and people jumping out of their seats to see the game better, she had dropped all the money out of her clothespin bag. She was standing there screaming and crying all at once, and no one was paying any attention to her.

Andy couldn't help but give a quick look toward the bleachers. Then, bang, something hit him on the shoulder, hard. He turned just in time to see what should have been a perfect fly ball rolling madly down toward the fence. By the time Andy had recovered the ball and thrown it home, not only had all the base runners come in, but Paddy Ryan had scored a home run as well.

"Hey, Taylor," yelled Jerry Margolis. "Who are you playing for, Westville or Midland Valley?"

Andy felt himself go hot with shame. Weenie turned around, and Andy pointed to the stands. By this time helpful people were gathering up Sally Jean's money.

"Never mind the popcorn," shouted Weenie. "Play ball!"

Andy nodded, and for the rest of the game he kept his eyes off what was happening in the stands, although it was hard not to worry about what those little Brownies were doing to his business. Fortunately Barry Lindhoffer hit a home run in the sixth inning with the bases loaded, winning the game for Westville by one run. Andy was never so relieved in his life. At least his team had not lost because of him.

After the game Mr. Coogan came over and asked Andy about his shoulder.

"It's okay," said Andy, although it was hurting a little.

"Better rub some liniment on it when you get home," said Mr. Coogan kindly. "By the way, what happened to you in the fifth inning?"

Andy told him about Sally Jean and the popcorn business.

Mr. Coogan scratched his head. "If I were you," he said, "I'd keep the popcorn business away from the ball field. Remember the old saying, 'Never mix business with pleasure'!"

Andy sighed. Mr. Coogan was right. It was pretty rough trying to manage a business from center field.

Movie
Business

THE MONDAY AFTER the ball game, the Taylor Popcorn Company held an important meeting at the apple tree. This business of selling the popcorn was becoming a real problem. It might be weeks before the people of the neighborhood were hungry for popcorn again. The Little League games were out. It wasn't fair to the team to have players with their minds on business instead of on that little round ball.

"Think," said Andy. "Think of a place where people like to eat popcorn."

"The circus," said Sally Jean promptly.

"There's no circus around here," replied her brother patiently. Sometimes he wondered how she could be so stupid and still walk around.

"I know," said Barry. "The movies."

"They already have a popcorn stand at the movies."

"Gosh," said Weenie, throwing a ball into the air and catching it, "that popcorn stand in the movies could use a little competition. They charge fifteen cents a bag, and we only charge ten cents."

"Yeah," said Jimmy Benson. "They have some nerve charging those prices."

"Maybe you have something there," said Andy thoughtfully. "There's no reason why we can't set up a stand *outside* the movies." The idea seemed better and better.

"Okay, partners," he decided. "Tomorrow afternoon . . . target, the Paradise Theater!"

The next afternoon the Taylor Popcorn Company gathered in front of the Paradise Theater just as the line of customers started to form, waiting for the doors to open. It was a hot day, and a lot of people wanted to go to the air-conditioned theater.

A monster movie was playing, plus two cartoons. It was a great day for the movies and a great day for popcorn.

The partners had cooked up a nice fresh batch of popcorn and had painted signs on their express wagons: "Why Pay More . . . 10¢ a Bag" and "Eat Taylor's — It's Tastier."

The girls went up and down the line with their clothespin-bag money sacks and baskets of popcorn while the boys hailed all the passers-by. "Nice fresh popcorn. Just made this morning. Buy at Taylor's cheap price!"

Business was wonderful. Practically everyone going into the movies stopped to buy a bag. After all, why should they pay fifteen cents inside when they could buy the same thing for ten cents outside? Barry and Weenie were shoveling in the dimes and feeling as happy as larks. They were sweating in the sun, but they didn't mind. The hotter it was, the more people would want to go to the movies.

Then the popcorn man from the theater lobby came out. He was wearing a white apron and a white hat with a red band around the edge. His face seemed even redder than the band around his hat.

For a few moments he just stood there with his hands on his hips and his jaw set, looking at the popcorn sellers. The boys felt all prickly down the back.

Then the popcorn man exploded. "Just what do you think you're doing?"

"Selling popcorn," said Andy meekly. He said it very quietly. One thing Andy's mother was fussy about — she did not like him to be rude to grownups. He was feeling rude inside though, and he was afraid it would show.

The popcorn man must have been able to see right through Andy. "Listen, you fresh kid," he said, "you have some nerve! I'm going to call the cops."

"It's a free country," yelled Weenie, who was so angry he forgot his manners. "What are you going to do about it?"

"Plenty," said the popcorn man, and he walked quickly down the street toward a policeman.

The policeman came back with the popcorn man. He looked at the partners. At first his face broke into a wide smile, for he was really a very cheery policeman with twinkly blue eyes. Then he swallowed and tried to look very stern.

"Look, fellows," he said. "I know that you are only trying to make a living. But there's a city rule against selling things on the sidewalk. You get in the way of traffic. You'd better pack up and sell your popcorn somewhere else."

Then, to show that his heart was in the right place, he put down a dime and took a bag of popcorn. "You're nice boys and girls," he said. "If they were all like you, we wouldn't have so much policing to do. Now do me a favor and move along before I get into trouble."

There was nothing to do but move the express carts away. After all, the policeman was the law, and you can't argue with the law.

The popcorn man stood there, glaring, and watched the partners pack up. Then he turned around and went back into the theater.

The partners walked slowly along the street, dragging their wagons behind them. No one said anything for a while. They were too discouraged.

Then Sally Jean pouted, "Forget that old movie. Let's start our own movies."

That was such a silly idea, everyone had to laugh, and then they felt better. They were still giggling a little when Andy stopped short. Everyone looked at him, wondering, as he held up his hand.

"Partners," he said, "my sister has come up with a million-dollar idea!"

"I did?" asked Sally Jean, surprised.

"Yes," said Andy. "I propose that the Taylor Popcorn Company go into show business. We'll give our own show and sell the popcorn between the acts."

Everyone started babbling at once. By the time the partners had reached the apple-tree conference place, ballet dancers and trick dogs and acrobatic acts were all mixed in a jumble of conversation.

Andy took his place on the second branch of the tree. He listened for a few minutes. Then he wrinkled his brow. One thing the popcorn business had taught him: you had to figure things out in advance before starting on a project.

"Just a minute," he said. "First, before we get started on this thing, where are we going to hold the show?"

The excitement simmered down to mumbles. A few of the group started to offer their basements. Then they remembered how their mothers had complained about using their kitchens for manufacturing the popcorn. They could just imagine what they'd say about a popcorn-selling show in the basement!

"I know!" said Barry finally, snapping his fingers. "The Henderson garage!"

"Let's Give a Show"

THE HENDERSON GARAGE was a most unusual place. It had not come with the Hendersons' house, but had been built by Mr. Henderson himself. And when Mr. Henderson built his garage, he had decided to make it extra large. He wanted a garage where one could put two cars, all the bicycles, the baby carriage, the lawnmower, the wheelbarrow, and the screens and storm windows, without crowding.

So Mr. Henderson built and built. He built the garage long. He built the garage wide. He built a giant garage. In fact, when he had finished, he no longer had to worry about where to put the lawnmower. He hardly had any lawn left!

Of course the Hendersons never did get around to putting the two cars, the bicycles, and the baby carriage into the garage. It was too full of children. It had been the meeting place for the Cub Scouts' Den 3, and it was a rainy-day gym for the whole neighborhood.

48

When the partners reached the Hendersons' house, they found Mrs. Henderson hanging up clothes on the line. Mrs. Henderson gave the children a friendly smile.

"Hi," she said. "What's up?"

"We want to give a show," said Andy breathlessly. "May we use your garage?"

"Certainly," replied Mrs. Henderson. "But don't forget. Make sure you have a clean-up committee."

"Oh sure," promised Andy. "We'll leave your garage better than new."

Mrs. Henderson went into the house, and the partners gathered in the garage to talk about the show. While they were talking, Mrs. Henderson's son Billy ambled in.

"What are you doing?" he asked.

"We're giving a show," explained Andy. "Do you want to be in it?"

"Okay," said Billy. "Say, did you see my new magic trick?"

He took some pennies and a handkerchief from his pocket. He tied the pennies in the handkerchief and then waved it around. Then he untied the handkerchief. Presto chango, the pennies were gone!

"Boy, you have real talent," admired the partners. "We need a magician for our show."

Billy stuffed the handkerchief back into his pocket. "I thought you were in the popcorn business. How come you're giving a show all of a sudden?"

"It's all part of the popcorn business," Andy told him. "You see, we're going to sell popcorn between the acts."

Billy looked down at one wiggling sneaker. "I'll bet you'll make lots of money."

"Hmmm. Maybe," said Andy. "We have to split it ten ways."

"You're using my garage," Billy reminded him.

"I know," said Andy. He frowned. Then he remembered Mr. Jensen from the five-and-ten-cent store. After all, this wasn't something they were doing just for fun. This was business.

"I'll tell you what, Billy," Andy offered, looking at his partners to see if they agreed. "Since we are using your garage, we'll give you a share in whatever money we earn at the show. Okay?"

The other partners nodded.

Billy smiled. "That's fair," he said.

Then, to make it a real business deal, Andy put out his hand and Billy shook it.

All that week the partners worked so hard on the show they didn't have time to make any popcorn. First they swept out the Hendersons' garage. Then they carried over chairs from all of their houses. Peggy Marshall's mother lent them two bedspreads to make a curtain. The girls pinned drapery hooks to the tops of the bedspreads, and the boys strung picture wire across the front of the garage on which to hang them. One side of the curtains had pink carnations and ruffles. The other side was decorated with Teddy bears (it was left over from when Peggy was a baby). It was a very interesting stage curtain.

As they sat in the front row of seats planning their show, it didn't seem as if they were in a garage at all. All the empty chairs and the curtain up front made it look like a real little theater. There was an exciting feeling that at any moment the show was about to begin.

But the show couldn't begin until they decided what to have in it.

All the girls wanted to be ballet dancers, and ran home to get their ballet slippers. Those who had leotards wore them, and those who didn't wore their bathing suits. All day they practiced turning and kicking and standing on their toes.

Jimmy Benson brought his clarinet and played "Home on the Range."

"We'd better put him at the end," Andy whispered to Barry. "It'll make the audience want to go home."

Billy Henderson found an old top hat and a cane. He drew a mustache on his face with charcoal and strutted around calling himself Hendo the Great.

Tommy Engel brought over his French poodle, Fifi, who was supposed to know tricks. She could walk on her hind legs if you held up her front paws.

Weenie showed how he could stand on his head for two minutes without wiggling.

Only Andy and Barry had no act. They wandered around wondering what to do. It looked as if everyone was talented but them.

Andy was trying to rewind the Henderson garden hose, which had fallen off the wall, when he accidentally knocked a dusty box off a shelf. Two cigar-box guitars fell out.

He ran over to the guitars and picked them up. "Hey, Barry, remember?"

Barry came over with a wide grin. "Sure. The Den 3 Strummers, at the pack meeting two years ago."

"Do you still remember the song?" Andy asked.

"I think so," said Barry. He sat down and slowly started to pick out "Alexander's Ragtime Band."

Andy followed him on the other guitar. They played louder and faster.

Weenie stopped practicing his acrobatic act and came over. "Say," he said, "Den 3 Strummers."

"Go into your dance, Weenie," shouted Andy and Barry.

Weenie moved his long legs and arms. "Come on and hear . . . ," he sang.

The guitars played and Weenie danced. Everyone gathered around and clapped. Then they all started to sing and dance with Weenie.

"Gosh," Andy laughed when the song was over. "Imagine. The Den 3 Strummers. I'd forgotten all about it. We've got to put this in our show."

It looked as if it was going to be a whale of a show. Now all they needed was an audience.

Fatima,
the Dancing Girl

THE POOR OLD APPLE TREE in the Taylors' yard was becoming crowded, for with Billy Henderson in the company, it had to hold six boys on its branches. They had to crowd together in some of the crotches to fit. The girls sat on the grass. Everyone was thinking. The problem was how to tell people about their show.

"Advertising," said Andy finally. "We have to advertise."

"An ad in the paper?" suggested Barry.

"Mmm, not bad. But expensive," Andy replied.

"I've got it!" shouted Weenie, jumping right out of the tree in his excitement. "We'll have a parade!"

"Yippee," yelled the partners. "A parade!"

Andy slid out of the tree. "We'll all parade our acts," he said. "Jimmy, your clarinet and the Den 3 Strummers will be the music. Tommy, you put a big bow around Fifi's collar and lead her on a leash. Billy, you dress up in your top hat."

"What about the girls?" asked Sally Jean.

Andy closed his eyes as if he were in a trance. "Don't stop me," he said. "I can see it. We'll put one girl in the express wagon. 'Come see Fatima, the beautiful dancing girl!'"

"Ooh," said the girls, all at once. Then, "I want to be Fatima."

"Wait, wait, girls. We'll draw lots," said Andy.

Bonnie Singleton shook her black hair and lifted her little nose up in the air. "I have a pink ballet costume."

"That's fine," said Andy. "The girl who is chosen Fatima will be able to wear it."

Bonnie shrugged her shoulders. "I won't lend my ballet costume. I want to be Fatima myself."

"That's not fair," said Sally Jean and Peggy and the other two girls. "We're going to draw lots."

"Maybe *you're* going to choose lots," Bonnie said, tossing her pony tail, "but *I'm* not. If I can't be Fatima, you can't have my costume and I won't help with the show, either."

"Don't be that way, Bonnie," said Andy, not quite knowing what to do.

"Oh, let her be Fatima. Who cares," said Sally Jean.

"All right," said Andy slowly. He still didn't think it was fair. But they were in a hurry. They didn't have time for quarrels.

Bonnie ran home with mincing little steps to get her costume. Sally Jean and Peggy wandered off to the grape arbor where they always told their secrets.

"Why did we let her?" exclaimed Peggy, tossing her braids.

"I don't know. She always makes such a fuss about everything," said Sally Jean unhappily.

"Well, she always gets her way," pouted Peggy. "And when we try to be fair, we lose."

Through the leaves of the grape arbor they saw the boys standing in a circle around Weenie. They were jumping and laughing.

Weenie was walking around like a girl. He put his hand on the back of his crew-cut hair, just the way Bonnie did. Then he snapped off a tree branch and flipped it up and down in back of his head like a pony tail. He ran around with bouncy little steps.

"If I can't be Fatima, I won't play," said Weenie in a high, squeaky voice. He drew his mouth down, imitating Bonnie, and wiggled his shoulders. "So there!"

The girls in the grape arbor giggled. Then they were quiet a moment.

Sally Jean said suddenly, "You know, I wouldn't want to be Bonnie Singleton. Not for anything."

The two girls smiled at each other. Then they held hands, glad that they were best friends, and ran across the lawn to the others.

The Big Show

I<small>T WAS A QUIET</small>, sleepy summer day in Westville. The sidewalks were empty. Everyone was just sitting around wondering what to do. It was too hot to play ball or to jump rope, and the children were all tired of sprinkling each other with garden hoses.

Then, all of a sudden, the sound of a screeching clarinet was heard coming around the corner. If you listened very carefully, you could make out "Home on the Range."

All the children and most of the mothers ran out to the street to find out the reason for the racket. They looked in the direction from which the music was coming and saw a strange parade.

First came Jimmy Benson puffing on his clarinet. He was followed by a group of girls whirling in their leotards and shaking tambourines made of paper plates and bottle tops.

Then followed a magnificent figure: Billy Henderson, wearing bathing trunks because of the heat, and a top hat. He was busy juggling three balls and chasing them when he missed.

Then came Miss Fifi Engel, glamorous in a big pink bow, led by her master. At this point all of Fifi's friends came dashing out, barking happily, and joined the parade too.

Next came an express wagon drawn by Weenie Jackson, who was shouting, "Come see Fatima, the beautiful dancing girl!"

Bonnie Singleton, all dressed up in her pink ballet costume, sat in the express wagon nodding and bowing and smiling to everyone, her pony tail flipping up and down. The original idea had been for Bonnie to stand on her toes, but she'd fallen down at the first bump, so she decided she'd better just sit down.

After that came Andy and Barry, playing "Alexander's Ragtime Band" on their guitars. They were wearing their Little League caps and carrying signs that read "Big Show This Afternoon, Hendersons' Garage," "Free Admission," and "Sponsored by Taylor's Popcorn, 10¢ a Bag."

All the children in the neighborhood stood on the sidewalk and clapped and cheered. Then they ran after the parade. By the time it reached Cherry Avenue, it was quite a sight! Dogs were barking, the clarinet screeching, the guitars going, the girls dancing, Weenie shouting, and all the children in the neighborhood running along behind.

The parade stopped in front of the Henderson house. Andy put down his guitar and made a speech. "That's all, folks. If you want to see more, come to Hendersons' garage at two o'clock. Admission is free, but don't forget to bring money for that delicious Taylor popcorn! It's tasty and nutritious. It gives you muscles!"

There was such a crowd at Hendersons' garage that afternoon that chairs had to be set up in the driveway. Before the show, the girls went around selling the popcorn. Business was good. Everyone was hungry. The bags of popcorn disappeared like a snowstorm in August.

Then Andy and Barry came onto the stage with their guitars. The popcorn sellers quickly put away the popcorn and ran up on the stage and started dancing to the music. At least they were dancing.

They kicked and they turned. Sometimes they turned in the wrong directions and almost kicked one another. Bonnie Singleton ran up to the front and balanced on her toes where everyone could see her. Sally Jean and Peggy did a duet in handsprings and nearly landed on the first row of the audience. Then all the dancing girls curtsied and threw kisses to the audience. The girls in the audience applauded and some of the boys booed.

Andy stepped forward. "There will be a brief intermission," he announced.

With that, the dancing girls rushed from the stage, grabbed their clothespin bags and popcorn, and walked up and down the aisle yelling, "Popcorn. Nice fresh popcorn."

Next on the program was Billy Henderson, who mystified everyone with his penny tricks and some handkerchiefs that became an American flag.

Then, there were the popcorn sellers again, this time begging, "*Please* buy more popcorn!"

After Fifi had done her act, walking on her hind legs and giving Tommy her paw, the audience started to groan when they saw the popcorn girls coming again.

"No more popcorn. We're dying of thirst. How about a drink?"

Some of the children in the audience started to get up and leave the garage. They were going to the Henderson house to ask for water.

"What'll we do?" Andy asked Barry in panic. "All that popcorn made everybody thirsty. We can't let this whole crowd go into Mrs. Henderson's kitchen, but if they don't get something to drink, they'll go home."

Just at that moment Mrs. Henderson appeared. She was carrying two large picnic jugs and a package of paper cups. She raised two fingers of her right hand in the Den Mother's "Quiet" sign.

"Everyone line up," she said. "Here's lemonade for all of you."

The partners helped Mrs. Henderson pass the lemonade. There was just enough to go around. Then everybody filed back into the garage and sat down. But it was clear that no one was going to buy any more popcorn. The audience had run out of money.

So the show continued without further intermissions. Weenie made a big hit with his acrobatic act. Then the Den 3 Strummers played all the songs they knew, and the audience sang along with them. Soon everyone was feeling so happy they even listened patiently while Jimmy Benson played "Home on the Range" on his clarinet. He sounded like a cross between a foghorn and a fire siren, but he got a good hand for trying so hard.

When the show was over and everyone had gone home, the partners gathered around as the girls emptied their clothespin bags of dimes. Andy counted the money. It came to nearly ten dollars, so he gave Billy Henderson ninety cents as his share.

After they had swept the popcorn out of Hendersons' garage and put away the chairs, the partners gathered over at the Taylors' house. They went into the garage and looked at the hundred-pound bag of

popcorn. It was not so fat any more. It had just a small bulge in the bottom. But the partners knew that that small bulge could make bags and bags of popcorn.

Weenie Jackson kicked the burlap bag with his toe. "Uh, Andy," he said, "I hope you won't think I'm running out on you, but I haven't been swimming in three weeks. Can I have my share of the money now?"

Then Barry Lindhoffer spoke up. "I'll have to quit too, Andy. My family is going away for two weeks."

Andy looked at the remaining popcorn. He was suddenly very weary. It would be nice to be able to enjoy the long vacation days without working so hard.

"Let's have a vote," he said. "All those in favor of breaking up the company, raise your hands."

One by one the hands went up. It looked as if everyone was tired.

"All right," said Andy. "We'll split the money now."

He went into the house and got the laundry bag in which he had been keeping the money. It was bulging with dimes. It looked like a fortune.

"It'll take us a year to count all those dimes," said Barry.

Andy scratched his head. "You're right." He thought a moment. "Let's take the money over to the bank and have them change it to dollars."

Profits

THE TELLER at the bank was astonished to see so many dimes. "Where did you children get so much money?" he asked.

"We earned it," said Andy proudly. "We had a popcorn business, but we don't feel like being in business any more. So we're dividing the money."

The teller's eyebrows rose with interest. "So you're liquidating, eh?"

"I guess so," said Andy. He had never heard the word before. "Yes, we're liquidating." He rolled the word around on his tongue. *Liquidating.*

The teller called another teller to help him. Their fingers flew among the dimes. Andy had never seen fingers move so fast. They counted once. Then they counted a second time to make sure they had the right amount.

"You have just fifty-five dollars here," said the teller, handing Andy eleven five-dollar bills.

Andy distributed the five-dollar bills among his partners. He had five dollars left over. He was about to ask the teller to change them into fifty-cent pieces so he could divide them, when Barry Lindhoffer spoke up.

"Andy, you keep the extra five dollars. After all, it was your popcorn."

"That's right," agreed the others. "It's only fair."

Andy looked at the two five-dollar bills in his hand. He'd never had ten dollars all at once before. He should have been excited. But he kept thinking of the $112.50 he had expected and the giant telescope he had planned to buy.

"What's the matter, sonny?" asked the teller. "Never saw anybody look so sad about ten dollars."

Andy's face reddened. "It's just . . ." he said, "it's just . . . when I first got the hundred-pound bag of popping corn, I figured on getting $112.50, sharing with my sister."

"Oh," said the teller, "lots of businessmen think they are going to make more than they really do." He took out a paper and pencil. "Let's find out what happened to all that money."

"Well," said Andy, thinking back to all the things that had happened. "In the beginning I figured on selling the popcorn for fifteen cents a bag, but we couldn't get enough customers, so we had to reduce the price to ten cents a bag."

"*Adjusting selling price,*" said the teller, writing. "Many new businesses have to lower their prices to get customers."

"Then," continued Andy, "We thought we'd get fifteen bags to the pound. But we burned a lot. It didn't come to more than eight bags a pound."

"*Spoilage,*" the teller wrote down. "Every manufacturer has to figure that in."

"Then I had to share the money with my partners. But I couldn't have sold the popcorn without them, either," Andy admitted.

"*Labor,*" the teller wrote down. "Always a large item. Were there any more expenses?"

Andy tried to remember. "We ran out of butter and oil, so we had to buy more. We bought cardboard and paint to make signs. We had to pay Billy Henderson ninety cents for using his garage. I guess that's about all."

Quickly the teller wrote down *Raw Material, Advertising,* and *Rent.*

"By the way," he asked, "did you start with any money?"

Andy told him about the ten dollars the partners had earned doing odd jobs.

The teller looked over the figures and whistled. "Boy!" he said. "Do you realize that your company made a profit of 450 per cent on its original investment? Why, that's amazing! Any businessman would be proud of that kind of operation."

After that, Andy didn't feel so disappointed any more about the ten dollars.

The partners walked out of the shadowy bank into the sunshine feeling very pleased with themselves. They all took out their money and looked at it. Somehow, these five-dollar bills looked different from any they had ever seen. They had earned every cent of them.

"Wait a minute," said Andy, struck by a thought. "Before we spend a dime, we have a debt. We have to pay Mrs. Henderson back for the lemonade and paper cups."

At first Mrs. Henderson would not take any money. "No, no," she said, "I can't take money for serving the children lemonade. I do that all the time."

"But this is business," Andy insisted.

"I'll tell you what," said Mrs. Henderson thoughtfully. "I don't want you to pay me any money. But I know a Cub Scout pack where the Cubs don't have much money. Their parents can't afford to buy them uniforms. What's worse, they have a hard time finding the money for their projects."

Andy looked around at his partners. Every boy there had once been a Cub. They remembered the good times they'd had in Mrs. Henderson's Den. There was no need to ask them what to do.

"Mrs. Henderson," said Andy, "we'd all like to chip in a dollar each for those Cub Scouts."

The Scientist

WHEN ANDY'S FRIENDS asked him to come along while they spent their money, he said he'd promised his mother to do some work around the house. Somehow he wanted to be alone. He wanted to do some hard thinking about the money he'd earned.

He took his nine dollars and walked slowly downtown with it. The stores were full of things you could buy for nine dollars. But Andy had to be very particular. He could not spend the money for which he had worked so hard on something that would break right away. He could not spend it on something that would get used up.

He went into a department store and asked to see telescopes. The clerk brought out a beauty. It was made of brass. Andy put it to his eyes and turned it. The clerk looked like a giant.

"You can really see the stars with that one," said the clerk.

"How much is it?" asked Andy.

"Twenty dollars," said the clerk.

"Oh," said Andy, disappointed. "I only have nine dollars."

The clerk smiled. "Well, if you're interested in science in general, not only astronomy, how about a microscope? I have a nice little beginner's microscope. Only eight-fifty. It's been marked down from ten dollars."

The clerk showed Andy how to put a glass slide and a little round cover glass under the microscope. He showed him how to adjust the eyepiece.

"May I look at something under the microscope?" Andy asked.

"Certainly," said the clerk. "Let's have one of your hairs."

Andy hastily plucked out a hair. The clerk helped him put it under the microscope. Andy stared in amazement. His little hair looked like the trunk of a tree! It even had knobs and lines on it.

"I'll buy the microscope," he said breathlessly.

Andy walked down Main Street with the microscope under his arm. But he was not really on Main Street. He was Dr. Andrew Taylor. He was standing in his laboratory, wearing a white coat. He had just discovered the Taylor Vaccine. The President of the United States was presenting him with a medal.

"I want nothing for myself," said Dr. Taylor. "I give my vaccine to humanity."

Andy shook his head and laughed a little. There he went again, dreaming about great big things. The

hundred-pound bag of popping corn had taught him how hard it was even to make part of a dream come true. But there was no harm in having a goal.

"Dr. Andrew Taylor," he said to himself as he came up the walk to his house. "The great scientist."

But first he had to start by being a little scientist.

He looked around for something to examine under his new microscope. There were so many things, it was hard to decide. A piece of grass, the inside of a flower, a leaf? He tried to think of what he wanted to know about more than anything in the world.

Then he ran into the garage as fast as his legs would carry him. He rushed over to the sagging burlap bag with its little bulge of popping corn. He reached into the bag and picked out one kernel of corn.

Carrying the kernel of corn and the microscope, Andy went up to his room. First he reached into his pocket and took out his remaining fifty cents. He slipped it into his college-education bank. Then he set up his microscope. He knew what his very first project as a scientist was going to be.

He was going to examine a piece of popping corn under the microscope. Perhaps he could answer a question that had been bothering him for some time. He was going to try to discover what made a kernel of popping corn pop.